OZZIE AND HA
BUILD A NEST

Written and Illustrated by

SHIRLEY RICHARDS

SBN: 153285871X
ISBN-13: 978-1532858710

G J Publishing
515 Cimarron Circle, Ste 323
Loudon, TN 37774
www.neilans.com

Dedicated to:

Ben

Grace

and

Harlan

Two bald eagles named Ozzie and Harriet
meet each other by a small pond at the edge of
a green forest.

They decide to build a nest, so begin looking
for a good tree with lots of spread out forks.

Ozzie begins the search for strong twigs on
the forest floor, and Harriet helps him.

Ozzie soon flies up to the tree, carrying one twig at a time in his claws or talons.

Both Ozzie and Harriet keep taking up twigs,
pieces of grass and other scraps to build the
nest in the open forks of the tree.

Finally, the nest is finished. It needs to be secure and strong because of the winds and rain. It is a big nest because bald eagles are big birds.

They both fly up and settle into the nest, side by side. It is here that Harriet will lay her eggs.

Harriet lays her first egg.

Three days later, Harriet lays her second egg. Bald eagle eggs are quite large and are white.

Harriet and Ozzie take turns keeping the eggs
warm, while the other forages for food for
this family of bald eagles.

Ozzie flies to a nearby lake and catches a fish in
his talons. He tears the fish into tiny chunks and then
feeds Harriet up in the nest.

Harriet and Ozzie share sitting on the eggs for a
month, keeping them warm and safe.

Finally, the big day arrives, and the first eaglet hatches. She pecks her way out of the shell. Her name is Gracie Girl, and she is a tiny bundle of soft gray feathery down.

x

Ozzie flies around to find fish or meat for the first
eaglet and Harriet. He tears the food apart with
his claws and feeds Gracie Girl with small chunks.

Now the second egg hatches, and here is Benjy.
He also is a soft, gray, down-covered eaglet.

Harriet leaves the nest to forage for food for herself. Ozzie keeps the eaglets warm.

Harriet takes the meat she finds from an old carcass lying on the ground, and flies it up to the eaglets.

Harriet and Ozzie take turns keeping the baby eaglets warm. Both parents forage for food for this family of bald eagles.

Today, Gracie Girl pokes her head over the side
of the nest which is high up in the tree.
Both Benjy and Gracie Girl are growing daily,
their parents feeding them lots of fish and meat.

After a month in the nest, both Benjy and Gracie
Girl are beginning to throw small sticks up in the
air from their nest. They play with the sticks as well.

After this game, they play tug of war with each
other. Another game to them.

Harriet and Ozzie take turns in the nest with both eaglets, while the other finds food.

Another month goes by, and, by now, both
Gracie Girl and Benjy are strong enough to
flap their wings while still in the nest.
The eaglets can also lift their feet from the
nest platform and rise into the air.

Harriet and Ozzie are often away from the nest now, perching on nearby stumps and branches.

When Gracie Girl and Benjy are around three
and a half months old, they flap their wings and
flutter to the ground safely.

They forage for their food, but still make their home in the nest.

While Harriet and Ozzie keep a look out for their eaglet
babies, the fledglings now wander all over
their forest home.

During the next four years, Benjy and Gracie Girl will grow full plumage and, one day, find their own bald eagle mates and build their own nests.

CPSIA information can be obtained
at www.ICGtesting.com
Printed in the USA
LVHW070820050520
654997LV00012B/2229

* 9 7 8 1 5 3 2 8 5 8 7 1 0 *